Billy Burger, Model Citizen is published by
Stone Arch Books,
A Capstone Imprint
1710 Roe Crest Drive
North Mankato, Minnesota 56003
www.mycapstone.com

Library of Congress Cataloging-in-Publication Data
Sazaklis, John, author.
  Recess is ruined / by John Sazaklis ; illustrated by Lee Robinson.
    pages cm. — (Billy Burger, model citizen)
  Summary: When a storm forces them inside for recess, third-grader Billy and his friends sneak
into the school library and turn it into a chaotic mess—so he organizes a book drive as an
apology.
  ISBN 978-1-4965-2588-8 (library binding)
  ISBN 978-1-4965-2685-4 (paperback)
  ISBN 978-1-4965-2689-2 (eBook pdf)
1. Book donations—Juvenile fiction. 2. School libraries—Juvenile fiction. 3. Elementary
schools—Juvenile fiction. 4. Families—Juvenile fiction. 5. Responsibility—Juvenile fiction.
[1. Behavior—Fiction. 2. Conduct of life—Fiction. 3. Libraries—Fiction. 4. Books and reading—
Fiction. 5. Schools—Fiction.] I. Robinson, Lee (Illustrator), illustrator. II. Title.
  PZ7.S27587Rc 2016
  813.6—dc23
  [Fic]   2015025094

Book design by: Ted Williams
Illustrations by: Lee Robinson
Photo credit: Mackenzie Bearup Photography, page 94

Printed in the United States of America in Stevens Point, Wisconsin.
092015   009222WZS16

Billy Burger
MODEL CITIZEN

RECESS IS RUINED

BY JOHN SAZAKLIS

STONE ARCH BOOKS
a capstone imprint

TABLE OF CONTENTS

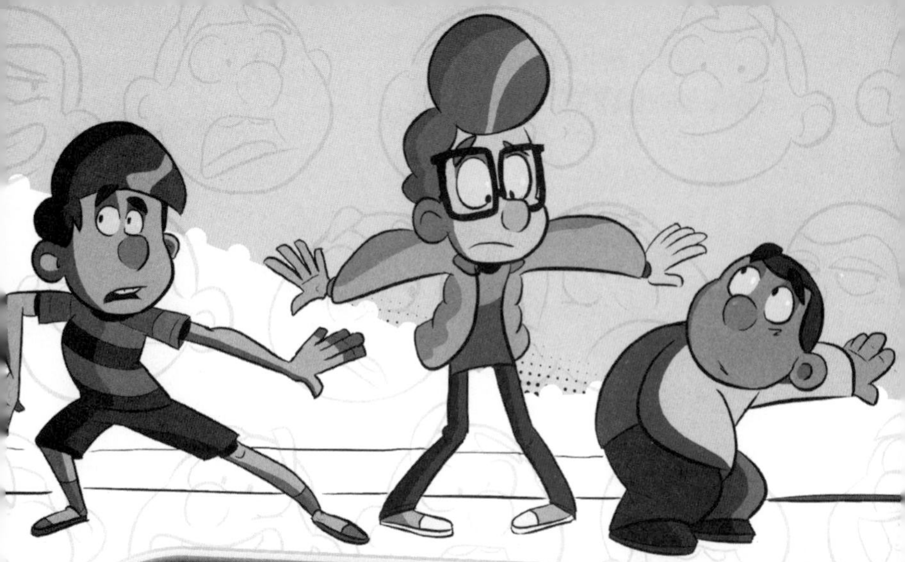

HEY, WHAT'S UP?

MY NAME IS
BILLY BURGER.

Nice to meet you! If you're reading this, you have good taste in books. Now that I know something about you, how about I tell you something about me?

I live with my family in a medium-sized house, in a little town called Hicksville, in the big state of New York. Our medium-sized house got much smaller the same time my family got a little bigger—when my baby sister, Ruby, was born. She's kind of cute . . . if you like stinky, smelly, noisemakers!

My parents both work at the Hicksville Police Department. Pretty cool, huh? Dad is a detective. Mom is a criminal psychologist. Together, they solve mysteries and catch troublemakers. Now that I think about it, that isn't much different than taking care of me!

But I wouldn't call myself a troublemaker, exactly. I prefer the term *adventurer*. I'm always looking for interesting things to do or discover because I get bored easily. I think it's because I have an overactive imagination.

(Want to know what's more overactive than my imagination? My appetite! I love to eat, and sometimes I think about that more than anything else. Seriously. I'll try anything . . . twice!)

I usually don't go on adventures alone. My partner in crime is also my best friend, Teddy. He lives a few houses down from me on the same block. I'm always trying to think of fun things for us to do together!

When I get an idea, it is usually awesomely epic. Unfortunately, my ideas don't always go as planned, and that's when I get in trouble.

But I'm working on that.

I'm working on being a better person, a better student, a better everything. Just like my grandpa, William Burger—the Hero of Hicksville. He's sort of a legend in our town. He did good deeds and inspired others to do the same.

And like Grandpa, I'm going to do just that.

I'm going to become **BILLY BURGER: MODEL CITIZEN!**

Cloudy with a Chance of Boogers

"All right, class, time for your science quiz!" says
Mr. Karas. The room responds with a series of groans
and moans.

Mr. Karas is my teacher. He's tall and has a beard.
Sometimes he brings his guitar to class to help us learn
with songs. Some of my classmates think he's weird, but I
think he's cool. And smart.

Hey, Mr. Karas, I think to myself. *For a smart guy, you're
pretty boneheaded when it comes to kids. We don't want to
take quizzes about precipitation! We want to play outside!*

I raise my hand to ask if we can go outside instead. Mr. Karas shoots me a serious stare before I even open my mouth.

"The answer is 'no,' Billy," he says.

WHOA! The dude must be a mind reader.

I lean over to my best friend, Teddy, sitting next to me and say, "I think Mr. Karas is a mind reader!"

Before Teddy can respond, Mr. Karas says, "A little less noise, please." He hands out a piece of paper to each of us.

But I can't be quiet.

Something inside me is bursting to get out.

"Mr. Karas," I say, without raising my hand. "I think we'd learn a lot more about precipitation if we went outside to study it. And the best place to do that is probably on the playground!"

Some of my classmates laugh at my joke.

Sal snorts, and a wet booger lands on his paper. It's green and slimy and it's glistening under the light.

"EWW!" shrieks Polly. "That's gross."

"Nice shot!" says Teddy.

"More like, nice *snot!*" I reply.

The class laughs.

Parker gets out of his seat so he can inspect the booger. He is so nosy! Parker is always sticking his big nose in other people's business.

"Bister Kadas, I need a new quiz," Sal says, holding the gooey paper.

"Yes, please throw that one away and come get a clean sheet," Mr. Karas tells him. "And please wash your hands!"

Then he turns to me.

"I'm in a good mood today, Billy, so I'm letting that little outburst slide *without* a warning," he says.

Then he gives me his serious stare.

Sal blows a snot rocket out of his nose and I'M the one with the outburst? I think to myself.

I look down at my desk and try to focus on the quiz. Then I look up at the clock.

No time has passed.

SAY WHAT?!

I raise my hand. "Mr. Karas, I think the clock is broken," I say.

He looks up at the clock and then down at his watch. Then he looks up at the clock again.

"It seems to be working just fine, Billy. Finish your quiz, please."

I stare at the clock for **ONE WHOLE MINUTE** without blinking. I want to make sure that the hands are actually moving.

Sixty seconds later, the hand moves. But I could swear it went backward!

"Mr. Karas!" I blurt out.

"Sounds good to me," Jason replies. "This time I get to be the Samurai leader. I won the coin toss, remember?"

"Oh, yeah," I say. "It's my turn to be the bad guy, Lord Pyros. I can take on all of you. Gimme your best shot!"

Suddenly—**KA-BOOM!**

There is a loud crash of thunder that makes everyone jump from fright.

I look out the window to see the dark clouds pouring sheets of rain all over the playground.

"Great," I grumble. "Recess is ruined."

This is the *second* time that precipitation has ruined my day.

Mission Impossible

TWEEET! The lunch monitor blows her whistle and announces that instead of going outside for recess, we will all go to the gym.

SAY WHAT?!

Going to the gym for recess is the worst. My friends and I can't play our superhero adventure games there. At least on the playground, no one pays attention to us. We can do whatever we want, no matter how babyish some other kids might think it is. (Especially Randy, the school bully, from Ms. Goodbinder's third-grade class.)

In the gym, we all have to play together. I'm just not in the mood for that.

NO, SIR!

Plus, Randy also plays rough and sends a lot of kids to the nurse's office.

NO, THANKS!

The four of us glumly watch the rain patter against the window. There is another flash of lightning and a crash of thunder. It makes me think of what we learned in science: When a lightning bolt travels from the cloud to the ground, it actually opens up a little hole in the air called a channel. Once the light is gone, the air falls back in and creates a sound wave that we hear as thunder.

"I don't know about you guys," Teddy says, "but I'm pretty sure that lightning and thunder are caused by the ancient gods clashing above the clouds."

"Whoa, did you read my mind, Teddy? I was just thinking about what we learned about lightning and thunder in science!" I say. "Clashing gods are definitely more awesome!"

"Can you imagine?" Jason says. "Zeus, Greek god of lightning, and Thor, Norse thunder god, blasting bolts at each other right over our heads!"

A lightbulb goes off over **MY** head.

"Why imagine when we can make it happen?" I say.

My friends look at me with puzzled expressions.

"What are you talking about? It just started raining and already you've gone cuckoo," Michael says.

"You won't think I'm crazy when you hear my idea," I say with a grin.

Then I lean in and whisper, "Do you want to get stuck in the gym playing team games against Raging Randy? Or do you want to play somewhere else by ourselves?"

"Go on," Teddy says.

I quickly tell my friends the plan I hatched in my head.

"You're right," Jason says. "You're not crazy. You're insane!"

"Don't be such a chicken," I tell him. "Now follow my lead!"

Once everyone gathers to exit the cafeteria, Jason, Michael, Teddy, and I stay at the back of the line.

We walk toward the gym, but when we get to the main hallway, I signal by cocking my head to the left. Finally we cut loose from the group.

We sneak down the hallway. Ducking under doorways so no teachers see us, we head toward the library. Once we get to our destination, I tell my friends to crouch low under the door.

"I'll sneak a peek and see if Ms. Blewski is at the desk," I say.

Ms. Blewski is the librarian. She's a little loopy and has really frizzy hair. It's pulled back into a tight bun that she holds in place with pencils and pens.

Sometimes the hair is so strong it rips loose. Those same pencils and pens shoot through the air like arrows! Ms. Blewski also wears really thick glasses. They make her look like an angry owl.

"Perfect timing, gentlemen," I say. "Blewski is taking her lunch break. Get ready to initiate Plan Alpha."

Michael reaches into his pocket and pulls out a pencil. He's always carrying one because he likes to draw. He's gonna be a famous artist for his cartoons someday!

The library door swings open, and we all take deep breaths and press against the wall.

Right as Blewski exits, it's Jason's turn. He throws Michael's pencil across the hall with an expert pitch. Jason could go to the World Series, he's so good at baseball!

CLANK!

The pencil hits the water fountain, catching the librarian's attention. She turns toward the sound and reaches up to her bun.

"Dear me," she says, walking after the pencil. "I must have lost another one!"

"She's lost something, all right," Teddy whispers.

The rest of us work hard to keep from laughing.

Once the librarian is a few feet away, I look at my friends and gesture toward the door. We hurry in before it shuts. Then we run and hide because the sound of her shoes clacking against the tile is getting louder.

Jason, Michael, and Teddy get all the good hiding spots behind the bookshelves. I have to rush across the room as the librarian reaches the door.

I duck low behind the giant globe next to her desk and hold my breath.

Ms. Blewski looks around the room one last time and locks the door behind her when she leaves.

We all quietly count to ten and come out of our hiding places.

"We're in!" Teddy cries.

"Let the games begin!" I reply.

4
Battle Royale

"WAH-HOO!" I yell. "We did it!"

The guys and I all slap high fives. "This is going to be an excellent adventure, Billy."

"Thanks, Teddy," I say.

Now that we're locked inside, no one will interrupt our radical version of recess.

Our creativity will be better than ever, because we can use the library's makerspace. There are so many different sections, we don't know where to begin! It's part science lab, part woodshop, part computer lab, *and* part art room.

All together, it's **COMPLETELY** awesome!

"So what are we waiting for?" Jason says. "Let's get ready to rumble!"

"Oh, yeah! Time for our Super Samurai showdown," Michael adds.

This is going to be awesomely epic!

"Okay, guys, here's the deal," I say. "Two of us get to be Super Samurai brothers and the other two get to be Zeus and Thor."

"Great idea," Michael says. "I'm Zeus!"

"Why do you get to be Zeus?" Teddy asks.

"Because I'm Greek. It just makes the most sense," Michael explains.

"Fine, I'm Super Samurai Galileo!" Teddy replies.

"Ooh, and I can be Super Samurai Nostradamus!" I shout.

"That means I'm Thor. Cool!" Jason exclaims.

Teddy and I run to the computer lab.

"This is going to be our headquarters," I exclaim. "From here, I can control the time portal that will make us history!"

"Wait, check this out!" Teddy cries.

Teddy is also kind of a computer genius. He hooks up Blewski's main computer to the projector and points it at the whiteboard.

Her screensaver of white stars and planets zooming through the universe is now the perfect backdrop to our space adventure.

"Dude," Jason says. "Great idea."

Teddy takes a bow, and Michael runs to the other end of the room.

"You'll never be able to storm the gates of Mount Olympus," he yells.

Another lightbulb goes off in my head. See? My imagination is always working in overdrive.

"Now we're talking," I say. I rub my hands together. "Let's build our battleground."

"Ooh, good idea," Teddy agrees.

"Find the biggest, fattest books," I say. "They are the sturdiest!" I pick one off the shelf and flip through it. A cloud of dust puffs out, and I start choking.

"ACK!" I wheeze. "What good are they if they don't have any pictures in them anyway?"

"Hey, I like reading books without pictures," Jason calls out.

"Good for you," I say with a smirk. "Maybe you and Ol' Blewski should get married. She can read you a bedtime story about the Trojan War."

"She can just tell him what happened since she was probably there," Teddy says.

"Ha-ha-ha!" Michael cackles. "Jason and Blewski sittin' in a tree . . ."

Then he makes smooching sounds with his lips.

"EWWW," Teddy says. "We just ate. You're gonna make me barf!"

"Let's go," I say. "Clock's ticking, dude. Let's make this the most epically awesome indoor recess ever!"

We take the bigger books off the shelves and start stacking two columns. Teddy and I work on one while Jason and Michael work on the other. When the books reach higher than our heads, Michael and I each stand on chairs to make the stacks a little taller.

From the art area, we each take a piece of construction paper, write our character's name on it, and tape it to a section of the room.

"Territory has been marked!" I announce.

"My dog pees on things to mark his territory," Jason says.

I laugh. "We are **NOT** peeing in the library!"

"And now it's time for the Super Samurai Showdown!" Michael shouts.

"Every man for himself!" Teddy cries.

Michael stands on top of a chair and hurls lightning bolts from above.

"ZAP! ZAP!" he says.

Teddy and I pick up an atlas and use it as a shield. Then we scurry behind the large rolling globe.

"This will be our Super Samurai spaceship," I tell Teddy. "At my signal, fire the proton beams at the gates of Olympus!"

"Aye, aye, Captain!" he says with a salute.

Jason rushes to the desk and picks up a ruler.

"This is mighty Mjölnir, the hammer of Thor!" he shouts. "Two can play this game!"

"Thor" hurls lighting back at "Zeus."

Michael hides behind the column of books. "**HA!** You missed!" he taunts.

I point at Michael and yell, **"READY, AIM, FIRE!"**

"Nothing is happening," Teddy complains. "The cannons are jammed, Captain. I must go outside and fix them."

"No, Galileo, stay inside the ship," I warn him.

Teddy doesn't listen and walks around to the other side of the globe.

"You're a sitting duck for Zeus!" Michael yells.

"ZAP!"

"Argh, I'm hit," cries Teddy. "This is the end of me!"

Teddy clutches his chest and heaves. Then he weaves around the room in circles.

Teddy is usually very dramatic. He wants to be an actor when he grows up. A while back he played Peter Pan in the school play and got a standing ovation!

Finally Teddy drapes himself over the globe.

"Nostradamus, my brother," he whispers. "You must avenge me. Combine our weapons for maximum damage upon the gates of Olympus!"

"Yes, Galileo," I say. "By Thor's hammer, I will avenge you!"

I roll the globe cart into the middle of the room and Jason jumps behind it.

"Join me, Thor, so that we may defeat Zeus once and for all!" I say.

"Olympus will be ours!" Jason yells.

We wheel closer to Michael and the stacks of books.

"Your puny spacecraft is no match for the lord of lightning!" he cries. "I shall smash it to smithereens!"

Michael hurls more bolts.

ZAP!

"Abandon ship!" I order Jason.

We leap out from behind the globe and run toward the stacks of books.

"Feel the might of my hammer!" Jason yells.

POW!

He punches one of the columns and it tips over.

SMASH!

Books clatter everywhere.

"**BAH**, is that the best you can do?" Michael yells.

"Here comes my Super Samurai combined weapon!" I shout. **"HI-YA!"**

BAM!

With a double-fisted punch, I knock over the second stack. The books teeter and topple and a really big, heavy one hits me on the head.

CLUNK!

"Ow!" I cry.

Teddy opens his eyes and starts laughing.

Michael walks over to me and says, "Looks like Olympus has fallen . . . on your head."

There is a sharp, throbbing pain in my forehead. **"OW,"** I moan again.

"Oh man, I wish I got that on video," Teddy says. "We could watch it again in slow motion . . ."

"It's not funny, guys. I think I'm really hurt," I say and pull my hands away. There's blood on them.

Jason comes over and says, "Oh, man. You're bleeding!"

"Does it look bad?" I ask. I can smell the coppery scent of blood.

"AHHH!" Teddy screams.

"Okay, nobody freak out," Michael says.

"AHHH!" Teddy screams again.

"We can fix this," Michael replies. "Stop screaming and go find something—anything—to stop the blood."

"It's just a scratch, right?" I ask.

"Yeah, don't stress out," Michael says.

But I don't believe him. Why would there be so much blood?

"It really hurts," I say.

"I'm sorry, buddy," says Michael. "If you were an action figure, you'd have true battle damage."

"Ha-ha, ow . . ." It hurts when I laugh.

Jason and Teddy rummage around in the librarian's desk and return with a plastic tube.

"How about this?" they ask.

I look at it closely.

"Lotion?! I'm bleeding, you fools," I say angrily. "I don't have dry skin."

"Oh, is that the one with the commercial where there's a lady sitting on a couch with a crocodile?" Michael asks, looking at the tube.

"Yeah," Jason and Teddy say.

Together, the three of them recite the commercial's slogan. "Feel like a crocodile? Tender Touch makes your skin smile!"

"Can we focus, please?" I snap. "My brains are oozing out of my head. I need medical attention!"

"Good idea, let's find a medical book!" Jason says, rummaging through the pile. "That'll help."

"Oh yeah, we can use the pages to absorb the blood!" Teddy adds.

My friends disappear behind the shelves, and I'm left all alone.

I sit down on the chair and hold my head.

I'm doomed, I say to myself.

Suddenly the door opens and Ms. Blewski enters.

"**BILLY BURGER!** What have you done to my library?" she shrieks.

Correction.

NOW I'm doomed.

5
Battle Damage

"Hey, Billy, I think we found something," Teddy calls from behind the shelves. My three friends rush over carrying a couple of books.

"Yeah, we didn't find any bandages, but we did find this book on mummies," Michael says.

I nod with my head toward the door.

Jason, Michael, and Teddy freeze in their tracks when they see Ol' Blewski.

"Well, Mr. Burger!" exclaims the librarian. "The puzzle pieces are falling into place now that I see *this* trio of troublemakers."

Falling, I think. *That's it!*

"We were walking along, minding our own business, when we heard all these books fall in the library," I reply.

"Yeah," Teddy says, catching my drift. "So, naturally, we came in here and tried to tidy up!"

"Of course!" I continue. "And then you arrived before we could surprise you!"

The librarian stares at us for a moment.

"That's quite a yarn, Mr. Burger. You must think I was born yesterday," she snarls.

"Oh, no, ma'am. Not yesterday," I manage to say.

"Yeah," Jason blurts out. "We know you were born a **LONG** time ago!"

I shoot him a look that says, *Keep your trap shut!*

"Enough jibber-jabber!" shouts the librarian. "All four of you are marching straight to the principal's office! I am shocked by this behavior. Such disregard for school property . . . and for books, no less! Books are the backbone of society! They are our friends!"

Our librarian's voice gets higher and higher like a steaming teakettle.

Then reality sets in.

My parents are going to be so mad at me if I get sent to the principal's office again.

My throbbing forehead reminds me that I have one last trick up my sleeve! It is every man for himself, after all.

"I can't go to the principal's office," I wail. "I need to go to the nurse! *Ohhh*, my head!!"

I lean back in the chair as if I'm going to faint. *Teddy isn't the only actor around here,* I think to myself.

The librarian walks to me and leans over to inspect my injury. She smells like the lotion. **UGH.**

"Hmm," she snorts. "I'll take you to see the nurse. And I'll have Principal Crank escort you to his office as soon as you're finished."

I gulp.

I'm already finished, I think. *If Crank calls my parents, my goose is cooked.*

Ms. Blewski marches us single file down the hall to the main office. She leaves Teddy, Michael, and Jason with Principal Crank's secretary.

Once we get to the nurse's office, the librarian barks, "Jackie, see to this one immediately! He's got an appointment with Principal Crank, and I don't want him to be late."

Nurse Jackie comes out from behind her desk and looks me over. She's a really nice lady with a warm smile and big brown eyes.

Nurse Jackie is actually kinda pretty.

"Hi, Billy," she says. "What happened?"

"I'll tell you what happened," blurts Blewski. "This troublemaker laid waste to my lovely library full of beautiful books!"

"Thank you, Ms. Blewski," Nurse Jackie says to the librarian. "I'll look after him now."

Blewski purses her lips and leaves the room. Then Nurse Jackie turns to me.

"It's a long story," I say.

The nurse pours some brown liquid onto a cotton ball. It smells funky.

"I'm going to put some iodine on the wound to disinfect it. It's going to sting a little, okay?" she says.

"Okay," I say.

The iodine does sting, but I try not to show it. I don't want Nurse Jackie thinking I'm a wimp.

When it dries off, she places a small bandage over it and says, "There, you'll be as good as new in no time."

Then she reaches into her drawer and pulls out a jar of candy.

My eyes go wide. There are lollipops with the gum in the middle and sour fruity chews and a few chocolate caramel swirls.

"SAY WHAT?!" I exclaim.

"I bet you've had a rough day, so I'm gonna let you have one, okay?"

Only *one?*

UGH.

I can't make such a difficult decision. My hands get clammy and I start to sweat. *Which one, which one?*

Finally, I close my eyes and reach into the jar. I grab hold of something and pull it out. It's the lollipop with the gum in the center.

Basically, it's a twofer. Two for the price of one.

SCORE!

"Thanks, Nurse Jackie!" I say as I unwrap the candy. "I should come visit you more often."

"Not if it means you get hurt," she says with a smile. I smile back.

"Would you like me to call your parents?" she asks.

"NO NEED," booms a voice that startles us both.

We turn to see Principal Crank standing in the doorway in his gray suit and gray shoes and gray hair. He looks like a big, grumpy rain cloud.

Suddenly, thunder rumbles outside.

"I have already called Mrs. Burger," Principal Crank explains. "Along with the parents of your classmates and cohorts."

My stomach does a flip.

Mom and Dad are usually disappointed in me after a call from Principal Crank. Then I have to try really hard to regain their trust.

"Your little visit to the library got you in **BIG** trouble, William. Now, follow me. You and I have much to discuss before your mother arrives."

I look over at Nurse Jackie. Her big eyes seem a little sad now.

I hang my head and follow the big, grumpy rain cloud back to his office. I wonder if I'll get struck by lightning.

Aftershock

By the time my head stops spinning, I'm in the car with my mom and we're going home. The windshield wipers sweep back and forth wiping the rain away.

Back and forth.

Swish-swoosh.

It's almost hypnotizing in a way. Then I start imagining myself hypnotizing Principal Crank next time I'm in his office. Once he's under my control, I'll make him cluck like a chicken!

"I just don't understand you, Billy," Mom says.

Mom is a criminal psychologist. She studies why criminals do what they do and tries to help them change their ways. With her help, they become better citizens.

When it comes to me, though, I think she's stumped.

"How many times do you have to get sent home before you learn from your mistakes?"

I shrug my shoulders.

"Are you not challenged enough at school?" she asks. "Are you acting out to get our attention? Help me understand, please."

I look down at my feet.

Mom keeps talking. "I know your father and I work a lot. And Ruby gets a lot more of my attention right now because she's a baby. That doesn't mean we love you any less. You know that, right?"

Mom used to work full time at the police station with Dad, but now she works part time so she can take care of Ruby during the day. Then Dad watches Ruby at night after his shift while Mom is with patients.

If no one is home to watch my baby sister, then they call in the big guns. That's what I call Grandma Burger. She's big and tough, but she's also really sweet. Plus, she gives me candy.

Thinking of Grandma makes me think of Grandpa. Grandma always tells me I'm a lot like him. *Rambunctious* is the word Grandma used to describe us. It means rowdy and wild.

"I just wanted to have fun during recess," I mumble. "That's all."

"You call destroying school property fun?" Mom asks, raising her voice.

"We didn't exactly destroy anything. We stacked some books, and they fell down. That's why they have hard covers—so they can take a beating. And I happen to know exactly how hard they are. One of them fell on my head."

"Then thank goodness you have a thick skull!" my mom snaps.

Well, she's right about that. I guess you can't fight with the facts. We ride the rest of the way in silence.

When we pull into the driveway, I see Grandma waiting for us in the living room window. She's holding Ruby and smiling. Ruby is holding one of her feet and trying to eat it.

"Your father will be home soon, and I have some time before my next patient to make dinner," my mom says. "Try and stay out of trouble until we discuss your behavior."

I get out of the car and kick a rock off the driveway. It bounces off the garage door and disappears in the grass.

I wish I could disappear too.

● ● ●

Grandma opens the door and greets us. Ruby starts to giggle excitedly when she sees Mom. Drool starts bubbling in the corners of her mouth and dribbles down her chin.

Babies sure have it easy. Sure, they pee and poop all over themselves, but they never have to go to the principal's office!

"Good afternoon, William," Grandma says.

"Good afternoon, Grandma," I reply.

Grandma says you should always address others formally when you greet them.

I tried it once and said, "Good afternoon, Theodore," to Teddy. He punched me in the arm.

He said that's what his mom and dad call him—and only when he gets in trouble. I'm assuming after Principal Crank's phone call earlier, my friend "Theodore" will be having a **BAD** afternoon instead of a good one.

Grandma bends down to kiss my forehead and then she greets my mother.

"Come inside, my dears," she says. "I already started working on dinner: My famous buffalo chicken and potatoes. Thought we could all use some comfort food."

"Oh, thank you so much!" Mom says to Grandma.

"I also boiled some water for a nice cup of tea," my grandmother adds.

Mom thanks her again, and then her expression turns serious.

"As you know, Billy's in some hot water himself," she says. "We have much to talk about tonight as soon as his father gets home."

"Indeed you do," Grandma replies. "But until then, let me have a moment with the boy."

We take off our shoes and Mom goes into the kitchen to make her tea. I follow Grandma into the living room. There is a blanket on the floor with Ruby's toys and baby things. Grandma sets Ruby down and then sits down next to her.

"Come here, William," Grandma says.

I sit next to her on the blanket.

Ruby crawls over to me and starts tugging on my socks. She tries to put *my* foot in her mouth, and Grandma pulls her away.

"Now, William," Grandma says. "Tell me everything."

And that's just what I do.

7
Secret Identities

After I tell Grandma what happened at school, she gives me a big hug. Then she asks, "Do you remember your grandfather, William?"

I nod my head yes.

My grandfather was the first William Burger, and I'm the second one that I know of. Grandpa died last year around the time Ruby was born. I'm named after him, in case you hadn't guessed it yet.

"William, your grandfather was a wonderful man. He was a loving husband and father and a decorated war hero. In short, your grandfather was a **MODEL CITIZEN**."

Grandma emphasizes the last two words. She usually gives me the same speech when I get in trouble, and I try really hard to let it sink in.

My grandfather was kind of a big deal. That's why he has a fountain with his name on it in the Hicksville town square.

It's right across from the library and near the train station. It was dedicated in his honor and is called the William Burger Reflecting Pool. Says so right on a marble plaque at the base. The fountain is really neat, and I visit it with my family all the time.

Sometimes Teddy and I throw coins in it to see our wishes come true. So far, I can't shoot laser beams out of my eyes and Teddy doesn't have a pet griffin. But we're not giving up yet!

"When your grandfather finished serving his country, he made sure that he continued serving by giving back to the community," Grandma continues. "He helped feed the hungry, shelter the homeless, and keep the neighborhood safe for children like you."

I know all of this already. Mom and Dad are always telling me to be on my best behavior and to set an example. To be a "model citizen," like Grandma said.

I look down at my socks and feel like I've let all of them down by being such a troublemaker.

"I'm sorry," I say quietly.

"My darling, do not feel bad or sad. I'm only reminding you that you carry not only your grandfather's name, but everything it stands for. You must honor both as best as you can."

Ruby gets fussy and crawls over to one of her board books. It's a story about a hungry caterpillar. She picks it up, squeals with joy, and hands it to me.

"No, thank you, Ruby," I say. "I'm cutting books out of my diet. They're bad for my health."

"Oh, what nonsense!" Grandma explains. "Books are wonderful and special things. They can take you on trips across the world and beyond the stars without ever having to leave the house. Books can fuel your imagination and educate you, so you can become a successful adult."

Oh, no, I think. *Grandma is starting to sound like Ol' Blewski!*

"Darling, not many people are lucky enough to have books. Did you know that your grandfather didn't even know how to read when he was a little boy?"

"Seriously?" I ask.

"Seriously," Grandma replies. "Not very many
people of our generation did. Going to school was
a luxury few of us could afford, because we were
working in fields, farms, and factories, just to get by."

Grandma pauses to make her point.

"Part of what made dear William so wonderful was
his determination and his hard work ethic. As a boy,
your grandfather would fill up his little red wagon with
scrap metal that he could trade in to get a few nickels
and dimes. Then he would spend the money on books.
Any books he could find. Especially comic books."

"Comic books?" I say. "I love comic books!"

"So did he," Grandma replies. "And he had the most
wonderful collection of all the greats: Spider-Man,
Captain America, Tarzan, and Zorro."

"Wow," I say. I still can't believe that Grandpa didn't
know how to read.

"You see, comic books taught your grandfather
how to read—with the help of his older brother, of
course," says Grandma. "But that was the start of his
love of books. It's a love that I also share. After all,
books are more powerful than a locomotive!"

"Ha! That's Superman, Grandma," I tell her.

"Oh, I know. Sweet child, I know." She pats my head, and I can't help but smile.

So my grandfather loved comic books too, huh?

I feel a little more connected with him now. I feel inspired. I want to do something good to make the Burger name proud.

"I guess books aren't so bad after all," I say. "Even the big, dusty ones without pictures."

"My precious, if it weren't for those big, dusty books full of information and knowledge, I don't think a man without super powers like Bruce Wayne would have been able to become Batman, you know."

SAY WHAT?! Grandma knows what's up!

"How do you know Bruce Wayne is really Batman?" I ask.

"Your grandfather wasn't the only one with a comic book collection," she says. Her eyes twinkle. "Now it's your turn to hit the books!" she adds. "A sharp mind equals a strong body."

"Thanks for the talk, Grandma," I say. "I'm going to make Grandpa proud and give back to the community. Just wait and see!"

I jump up and gather my school stuff from the hallway. Just then, the door opens and Dad walks in. He looks tired and grumpy, just like Principal Crank. Must be a grown-up thing.

But I'm so pumped up with energy, I forget that I'm still in trouble.

"Hello, family," Dad says to us. Then he goes into the kitchen. "Hello, my beautiful wife." He kisses Mom on the lips. I shut my eyes because it's so gross.

"I hear we need to have another discussion about Billy's behavior," he says, plopping down on a chair. "You know, son, sometimes you're more of a handful than the criminals I put in jail. Go to your room until Mom and I figure out our plan for punishment."

"Gladly!" I say with a big smile.

My parents give each other confused looks as I rush into my room.

Usually I put up a fight, but not this time.

This time, I have a plan too!

8
Man with a Plan

Once I am alone in my room, I chuck my schoolbag
onto the bed. Then I walk over to my bookshelves.
Looking at them closely, I realize that I have a lot
of books.

Grandma's right. It's easy to take things for granted
if they are always around you. Soon you start to forget
they are there. It's been a while since I read some of
these. Plus, a few of them are kinda babyish. I think it's
time to let them go and find a new home.

That's my plan.

I'm going to collect old and used books and donate them to people who aren't as lucky to have a collection of their own.

I grab a stack of books off the shelf and place them on my floor. I repeat this a few times until all my books are off the shelf and in stacks around me. This gives me a flashback to the school library earlier today, and my forehead starts to throb.

I touch my bandage and wince from the pain. *Focus, Billy,* I tell myself. *Wait for it to scab over, then pick at it. Now is too soon.*

I sit in the middle of the stacks and start looking through each book, one by one.

I make three piles: **YES**, **NO**, and **MAYBE**.

YES books I'm definitely keeping.

NO books are babyish or no fun and have to go.

MAYBE books I can hold on to and share with Ruby when she's older.

In the **YES** pile go all of my books about outer space and Samurai. I got most of them after I started watching *Super Samurai from Outer Space*. I wanted to learn more about our solar system and the ancient Japanese warriors.

I'm also keeping my books on ancient Egypt, Greek mythology, and marine life. Oh, and these word search and hidden picture puzzle books. I'm not finished with them yet!

In the **NO** pile, I'm putting some old picture books from when I was younger. Especially this depressing one about a tree that lets a spoiled brat cut it down. **YEESH!**

I come across two of my favorite picture books and smile when I look at the covers. One of them, about a fat bear that gets stuck in a honey tree, I made Mom read to me every night because it was funny.

The other one, about a tin soldier with one leg who goes on an adventure, I had Dad read to me because it was exciting.

I look at them one last time before putting them on the **YES** pile. This pile is significantly bigger than my **NO** pile.

Hmm . . . letting go of books is a lot harder than I thought.

Finally I come across some unused coloring and activity books that I got from my Uncle Cliff and Aunt Claire. These I can donate for a good cause.

Then I start rifling through my comic books. *Okay*, I tell myself, *time to get tough. Keep the awesome ones, and let the less awesome ones go. Maybe some kid will find them to be more awesome than I did.*

Grandma sometimes says one man's trash is another man's treasure. Well, now I know what she means by that!

I stand up and take a deep breath. My giveaway pile is pretty decent looking.

Not bad, Burger, I think to myself.

KNOCK-KNOCK.

Someone is at the door. I open it to see Mom and Dad.

"Are you ready to discuss your—" Mom stops when she sees my room. **"GOOD GRACIOUS! WHAT HAPPENED IN HERE?"**

"Looks like a tornado blew through, Billy," Dad says as he looks at my stacks.

"It's all part of my plan," I tell them. But I can see my parents growing impatient.

"Make it fast, Billy," Mom says.

I quickly tell them about my idea about donating books to those who need them. Their eyes go wide with surprise.

"I'm impressed," Dad says.

Mom smiles and kisses me on the head. "That's a great idea, Billy." Then she adds, "I'm sure if your father and I go through our shelves, we'll find some books to add to the collection."

"Oh, yeah," adds my father. "The garage has boxes of textbooks and manuals and magazines that we don't need anymore. I'm thinking we can bring them all to the Hicksville Public Library."

"Yes, that garage could certainly use a cleaning, as I'm often reminding you, dear," Mom says to Dad.

"Duly noted," replies my father. He kisses Mom again.

"BELCH!" I say, gagging. "No time for love, dudes! We need to share the wealth! We need to help our fellow man! We need to drive to the library right now! We need to—"

"Take a chill pill, *dude*," Dad says. "You're still in big trouble."

"I know that Dad, but I'm just so pumped," I tell them. "Grandma told me all about how Grandpa couldn't read as a kid. I realized I've taken my books for granted."

"Good, because they can keep you company when you're not watching TV and playing video games for a week," Mom says.

"Fine by me!" I exclaim. "Who needs that stuff when you've got books?"

Mom and Dad stare at each other again.

"Who is this child?" Mom asks.

"I don't know," Dad replies. "But can we keep him?"

9
Billy Burger Book Drive

The next day, I meet Teddy at the bus stop at the end of our block. He asks about my head. I say it's getting much better.

"So what did your parents say?" I ask him.

"No TV and video games," he replies. "Yours?"

"Same," I say.

"Oh, man," Teddy says. "That's rough."

"Eh, it's not so bad," I shrug.

"SAY WHAT!?" Teddy exclaims.

I smile at him.

"**JEEZ**, Billy, you must have hit your head harder than you thought. You're talking crazy," says Teddy.

The bus arrives, and Teddy and I climb aboard.

As we walk toward the back, my stomach starts to sink. Randy stands up and shouts, "Well, if it isn't the rest of the Library Losers!"

All the kids on the bus laugh.

Normally, I would stand up to Randy and tell him to go take a long walk off a short cliff, but this time I'm taking the higher road.

Teddy and I push past him and find Michael and Jason sitting a few seats from the back.

"So . . . Library Losers, huh?" I ask.

"Yeah, that's what they're calling us now," Michael says with a shrug.

"Word sure travels fast," adds Jason.

We sit in silence staring out the window when a head peeks around the seat in front of us.

It's Parker, ready to nose around.

"So what happened at the library?" he asks.

"We wanted to check out some books. What do you care?" I snap.

"Looks like the books checked you into the nurse's office. Ha-ha-ha!" Parker laughs.

"Ha-ha, you're so funny," Polly says to Parker. She gives us a dirty look.

"Yeah, he's funny," I add. "Funny *looking*."

"Nice one," Teddy says.

We bump fists.

"Yeah, serves him right," Michael adds.

"You're nothing but a big troublemaker, Billy Burger," Polly huffs and flips her hair in my face.

I lean back in my chair and cross my arms over my chest.

"We'll just see about that," I mumble back.

● ● ●

When we get to school, Teddy, Jason, Michael, and I are met with stares and whispers and all-out pointing from the other students.

The old me would have gotten angry and wanted to pick a fight. But the new me feels surprisingly cool and calm.

"Just ignore them," I tell my friends.

Jason and Michael exchange looks.

"Billy, are you feeling alright?" they ask.

"He hasn't been the same since he got conked on the head," says Teddy.

"Maybe we'll need to hit him again with a bigger book to get him back to normal?" Jason suggests.

I smile and say, "I'm fine, really!"

When we finally get to our classroom, I tell Teddy and the guys what I did last night. I had been itching to tell them all morning, but we hadn't had any time alone.

When I get to the end, I say, "By the time my family and I finished sorting through our books, we each had a cardboard box full of them."

"So what did you do with them?" Teddy asks.

"My dad drove us to the public library, and we gave them to the librarian. She was so excited. I thought *her* bun was gonna pop off like Ms. Blewski's. She said they were going to put the ones in good condition on the shelf. Any doubles or slightly damaged ones will go on the sale tray to help raise money for the library."

"You're like . . . a saint!" Teddy says. "Saint Burger!"

"Ha! Nah," I say coolly, "just doing my part to give a little back. It's what my grandfather would have done. He was a model citizen."

Suddenly a deep voice interrupts us.

"What an excellent story!"

SAY WHAT?!

I turn around to find Mr. Karas standing over us.

"I couldn't help but overhear what you said, Billy,"
says Mr. Karas. Then he claps his hands until the room
is quiet.

"Listen up, class. You could learn something from
Billy Burger."

"We can?" Parker sniffs in surprise.

"We most certainly can," says Mr. Karas. "Billy's
recent actions make him . . . dare I say . . . a **MODEL
CITIZEN**," says Mr. Karas. "Billy is someone to look
up to!"

Polly's mouth drops open.

"He is teaching us that if we're fortunate to have nice
things like books, then we can share them with others.
And reading is the first step to becoming successful
adults. By the end of the week, I want you to bring in
any old, used, and discarded books. We're having what I
am officially calling the **BILLY BURGER BOOK DRIVE**!"

The whole class is staring at me in disbelief.

Is this really happening? I think to myself. *This feels awesome. I've never had anything named after me. This has to be a step closer to being a model citizen!*

"This is working out great, huh?" Teddy says.

"Yeah, I'm feeling pretty psyched, dude," I reply.

"Don't get used to it," huffs Polly. "You'll probably mess up again real soon, I'm sure."

"Oh, stuff it, Polly!" I snap. I can't help it.

The class laughs at my response and Polly's face turns beet red.

Mr. Karas writes my name on the board and shakes his head. "That's strike one, Burger. And you were doing so well."

"First and last one, sir. I promise," I tell the teacher.

Then I lean back and smile at Polly.

"Totally worth it," I say.

10
It's Not a Barbecue

As the days go by, the other students and I bring in our books for the Billy Burger Book Drive.

I just love saying those words: *The Billy Burger Book Drive*.

It's the first thing I've ever had named after me. It may not be a fountain like Grandpa, but it's only the beginning.

Mr. Karas set a big cardboard box next to his desk for our books. Slowly but surely, the box began to fill up.

Each day I would use the pencil sharpener several times so I could get up and glance inside the box. I liked seeing it fill up.

The class was taking part in a good cause that I started. And that felt awesome.

Now Friday is finally here. It's the last day of the book drive.

"Please come up one by one, and drop off your final donations," Mr. Karas says.

I stretch my body from my seat to see what everyone brought in. It looks like a lot more books since the day before. **AWESOME!**

I see that Michael brought in some books about art. Jason brought in some books about sports. Sal, with all his sneezing, brought in a book about allergies.

I brought in all the books from my **MAYBE** pile, since my **NO** books already went to the public library.

When we finish, Mr. Karas counts the books.

"Well, well," he says. "We can officially call the Billy Burger Book Drive a success!"

"YES!" I shout.

"We have eighty-six books! Impressive. I will add to the collection and make it an even hundred."

"WOO-HOO!" I shout again. The class cheers and claps their hands. I high-five Teddy.

Then I remember to raise my hand and wait for Mr. Karas to call on me.

"What are we going to do with the books?" I ask.

"That's an excellent question, Billy," says Mr. Karas. "Does anyone have any ideas?"

Polly raises her hand first. "We can read the books to the other grades," she says.

"Excellent idea, Polly," Mr. Karas says.

Teddy raises his hand. "I've got a better idea! We can act out the parts and put on little plays!"

"Ever the showman, Teddy," Mr. Karas replies.

Teddy stands up and takes a bow.

Parker raises his hand next and says, "We could stand them upright and create a maze for Franklin our ferret to crawl through!"

"While that is an excellent suggestion, I think that it's best if we focus on—"

"AAAAHHHH!"

A loud scream interrupts Mr. Karas. It came from the hallway. We all jump from our seats.

"Everyone stay back and stay calm," Mr. Karas says.

He opens the door and steps into the hallway. The smell of smoke wafts into our noses.

"Is someone having a barbeque?" I ask. My mouth starts to water.

"No, Billy," says the teacher. "Where there's smoke, there is usually a fire."

BEEP! BEEP! BEEP!

Suddenly the fire alarm goes off.

"Yup," says Teddy. "There's a fire!"

The class starts talking excitedly, and Mr. Karas whistles loudly to get our attention.

"Okay, class, you know the drill. Single file out the door, straight to the playground. No talking, and stay close to each other."

We follow his instructions. Mr. Karas waits for all of us to exit before scooping up our class ferret, Franklin, from his cage and then shutting the classroom door.

Ahead of us is Ms. Goodbinder's third-grade class. Many of the students are coughing and covering their faces. They look scared, but no one seems to be hurt.

The smoke is coming out of their classroom.

Teddy and I crane our necks backward as we see someone running back into the room.

"Oh, man, did you see that?" I say.

"Yeah, somebody ran back into the classroom!" Teddy replies.

"Billy, please face forward and no talking," orders Mr. Karas.

Once everyone is outside, Mr. Karas takes attendance. I look around. The whole school is standing in the front yard. Luckily, it's just cloudy and not too cold. It feels weird being on the playground and not wanting to play.

I can still smell the smoke. It must be stuck in my nostrils.

I've never been near a real fire before. Even though I didn't actually see it, I'm imagining it as being really big and orange and hot like in the movies.

Then I start thinking about the person who ran into the classroom.

Who was it?

Why did they do it?

WHAT WILL HAPPEN NEXT?

From Loser to Legend

WHEE-OOH! WHEE-OOH!

Suddenly there are loud sirens and bright lights. A fire truck pulls into the school's parking lot. The firefighters hop off and rush into the building.

"Whoa," Michael says.

I point at them and say, "Did you see their cool gear?"

"Dude, that guy's got an axe!" Jason exclaims.

"COOL!" Teddy cries.

Moments later, Principal Crank comes out with Joe, our custodian. Mr. Crank looks grumpier than usual.

"May I have your attention, please?" Crank says, raising his hands.

A quick hush falls over the crowd.

Crank clears his throat and says, "The fire chief informs me that the fire was caused by a faulty electrical outlet that the fire department is currently investigating. We won't be able to re-enter the school until their investigation is complete."

Everyone murmurs and whispers to each other and the principal raises his hands once again for silence.

"Luckily and thankfully, the fire was extinguished in time by Mr. Phillips, our crafty and clever custodian! He managed to fight the blaze and put it out before it spread to the rest of the classroom. I think we all owe this hero a great big thanks."

"YO, JOE!" I yell and start clapping really loudly. "He really is a hero. Way to go!"

There are cheers and applause all around.

The custodian smiles and nods his head. "Just doin' my duty," he says. Then he walks over and takes Ms. Goodbinder's hand. "I'm sorry about your room."

"Thank you, Joe. I really appreciate your help," she says. "The most important thing is that everyone is safe."

"It's sad to say this, but that fire extinguisher did more damage than the fire. That little book nook of yours is in really bad shape, Ms. G," Joe adds.

"How bad?" the teacher asks.

"Your books are ruined," the custodian tells her.

Ms. Goodbinder gasps.

"That's great!" I exclaim.

"Billy!" Mr. Karas says, surprised.

"BURGER!" Principal Crank growls.

"No, wait, don't you see?" I ask. "Now we can use the Billy Burger Book Drive to help Ms. Goodbinder and her class!"

● ● ●

After what seems like five hundred forevers, the fire chief tells Principal Crank that we can go back into the school.

The principal also announces that, "in light of the day's events, there will be early dismissal." The main office is currently contacting our parents.

Each classroom files into the building one after the other. Mr. Karas's class follows Ms. Goodbinder's up the main hallway and to the left.

The smell of smoke is still in the air. It gets stronger as we get closer.

I walk to the head of our line and tap Mr. Karas on the shoulder. He turns around and asks, "What is it, Billy?"

"Did you give any thought to my idea?" I ask him.

Mr. Karas stares at me blankly. It looks like the lights are on, but nobody's home. "What idea, Billy?"

"About helping out Ms. Goodbinder's class with the Billy Burger Book Drive?"

"Oh, right," he says, handing me Franklin. "Would you mind holding the ferret, I'm a little distracted at the moment. Let's discuss when we are all in our room."

As we reach our classroom, I watch Ms. Goodbinder and her students enter theirs. I sneak over to the room and look inside. In the far corner there is a black, charred mess where Ms. Goodbinder used to have her book nook.

It looks so sad.

I rush back to our classroom and put Franklin in his cage. Then I stand next to Mr. Karas and clear my throat.

"Ahem," I say, nodding toward the books.

Mr. Karas looks at me and smiles. "It seems that Billy Burger has had another brilliant idea. How many of you are in favor of donating all the books we collected to Ms. Goodbinder's classroom? Let's see a show of hands."

Surprisingly, everyone in the class holds up their hand. Including Polly.

Teddy holds up both hands.

"Then it's unanimous," Mr. Karas says. "Let's go pay the other third graders a visit, shall we?"

He picks up the big box of books, and we follow him into the hall. I knock on Ms. Goodbinder's door and ask if we can come in.

"Please do," she says as she opens the windows. "We could use some extra company."

Our class squeezes into Ms. Goodbinder's room and stands against the wall. A lot of the kids cover their noses with their shirts to block out the smoke smell.

Randy sees me and my friends and says, "Hey, look, it's the Library Losers!"

A few of his friends laugh, and Ms. Goodbinder shoots them a look. "Randall, that's a warning!"

Randy shuts his mouth and sneers at me.

"We are truly sorry for what happened to your room," Mr. Karas says. "And we hope that this little gesture goes a long way. On behalf of our class, we would like to donate the books we collected for the **BILLY BURGER BOOK DRIVE** to you!"

Mr. Karas places the box on the floor, and the kids all move closer to have a look inside.

"Oh, wow!" Ms. Goodbinder says. "I'm speechless . . . what is the Billy Burger Book Drive?"

Here's my moment to shine, I think to myself.

"Well, you see, Ms. Goodbinder," I say. "After I got some sense knocked into me, I realized that books are very special and important. We should appreciate them. So I collected some old books from my house and donated them to the library so I could prove to my parents that I can be a model citizen. Then Mr. Karas had the idea that we should **ALL** collect books in his class. We filled up this box, but we didn't know where to donate them . . . until we saw you needed them."

Ms. Goodbinder's eyes well up.

"That is the sweetest thing anyone has ever done," she sniffs. "I guess every cloud has a silver lining after all!"

"They do?" I ask. "Hey, Mr. Karas, was that on the precipitation quiz?"

Mr. Karas laughs. "No, Billy, that means that something good can always be found in a bad situation."

"Hey, that's kind of like what happened with us at the library," I say to my friends.

"And speaking of libraries," Ms. Goodbinder continues, "I am on the library committee along with Ms. Blewski. I'm going to tell her that I'd like to make this week the Billy Burger Book Drive week every year!"

"SAY WHAT?!" I exclaim.

"Congratulations, Billy," Mr. Karas says. "That's quite an honor!"

"Dude, you're famous," Teddy says. "Way to go!"

I'm pretty jazzed up. It feels good to do good!

I feel like I made Grandpa proud.

And I feel like I made Mom and Dad and Grandma proud too.

Maybe they'll admit that being rambunctious can sometimes be good . . . or at least lead to good things when you learn from your mistakes.

Another great thing I realized? One day little Ruby will grow up and collect her own books for the Billy Burger Book Drive.

I close my eyes and let it all sink in. Yep. It still feels really good.

"This Library Loser is now a Library Legend," I say.

And everyone agrees.

About the Author

New York Times best-selling author John Sazaklis enjoys writing children's books about his favorite characters. He has also illustrated Spider-Man books and created toys used in *MAD Magazine*. To him, it's a dream come true! John lives with his family in New York City.

About the Illustrator

Lee Robinson grew up in a small town in England. As a child, he wasn't a strong reader, but the art in books always caught his eye. He loved to see how the characters came to life. He decided to become an illustrator so he could create worlds of characters himself. In addition to illustrating books and comic books, Lee runs workshops to help teach kids about literacy, art, and creativity through comics.

WHAT DO YOU THINK?

QUESTIONS TO THINK, TALK, AND WRITE ABOUT

1. What is a model citizen? Do you know a model citizen? Write about him or her.

2. Choose two characters from the book and list five words or phrases to describe each of them. Then compare the two characters. How are they alike? In what ways are they different?

3. Imagine that Billy and his friends were transported to the gates of Olympus. Write a short story about their adventure.

4. How do Billy's parents feel when they discover him going through his books? Use details from the book to support your answer.

5. Write about a way that you could help others. What resources would you need? Are there people who could help you?

Billy's Glossary

avenge—to get back at someone for something bad they have done

awesome—very, very cool, like me and my friends and the Super Samurai

backbone of society—the thing that the future is built on, though I'm not sure how you build a future on books

behavior—how you act; Sometimes I have slightly bad behavior, but other times my behavior is that of a model citizen

cohorts—the kids you get in trouble with

creativity—the ability to come up with epically awesome ideas and make epically awesome stuff

dedicated—put someone's name on something in their honor; Now both William Burgers have something dedicated to them: Grandpa's fountain and my book drive

determination—a strong and steady plan to do something; The Super Samurai have loads of determination

disregard—pay no attention to; It would probably be a good idea to disregard Randy more often

epic—super awesome; Probably more awesome than anything you've ever seen

generation—a group of people who were all born around the same time; Thankfully, MY generation has video games, unlike my grandma's generation

luxury—something that is awesome to have even though you don't really need it

meteorite—a piece of rock or metal that falls from space

precipitation—a long word for water that comes from the sky; It could be rain, snow, sleet, hail, and maybe even sweat from the gods

projector—a cool machine that makes slides or movies bigger and puts them up on a screen

smithereens—tiny little pieces; I bet Randy wishes he could break the whole third grade into smithereens

standing ovation—when an audience stands up and cheers and claps after an awesome performance

startles—surprises in a not-so-great way

territory—a certain area; Note: stay out of enemy territory

unanimous—when everyone agrees on the same thing

universe—everything in space; We're talking the planets, stars, moons . . . you get the picture

work ethic—how hard you work; You can be lazy and have a poor work ethic, or you can be hardworking and have a great one

BENJAMIN BEARUP

A REAL-LIFE MODEL CITIZEN

Teenager Benjamin Bearup started volunteering with Sheltering Books, Inc., in 2008. This organization, which was started by Benjamin's sister, is like a never-ending book drive. Volunteers collect books to donate to people in homeless shelters and other short-term homes. So far the organization has donated 360,000 children's books to shelters in 45 states and six countries!

Benjamin got involved after he helped deliver some books to children at a homeless shelter. **"I SAW HOW GRATEFUL THEY WERE TO GET THE BOOKS AND REALIZED THEY ARE GREAT KIDS AND ARE JUST LIKE YOU AND ME,"** said Benjamin.

This real-life model citizen helps collect books, makes sure they are in good shape, and gets the right type of books to the right shelters. "We wouldn't want to send books that mainly girls would like, to an all-boys shelter," he explains.

For readers who want to make a difference, Benjamin suggests finding something you love and sharing it with others.

"If you love to read, then a book drive might be a good choice. If you love animals, then holding a pet food drive or collecting old blankets and towels for a shelter will be a fun activity for you. If you love sports, hold a used sports equipment drive. There are lots of fun options that fit everyone. You will have fun helping others!"

For more information on Sheltering Books, Inc., visit www.shelteringbooks.org

"That's it, Billy Burger. No more Mr. Nice Teacher," Mr. Karas says with a frown. "I'm writing your name on the board."

That's one strike against me. Two more strikes and I get sent straight to Principal Crank's office.

As the teacher writes my name, I stare at the clock and curse it.

"I hope you fall off the wall," I whisper.

I return to my quiz and try not to think about lunch and playing on the playground. I have learned that time at school actually passes faster when you're focused on your work. If you stare out the window and daydream, time stands still.

I tend to stare out the window and daydream **A LOT**.

It's just that the playground is **RIGHT THERE**. And I would rather be playing on it **RIGHT NOW**, instead of being stuck inside doing schoolwork.

But no matter what, we're going to be stuck inside until Mr. Karas lets us out for lunch.

What if I die of starvation before then?

2
Lunch Rush

Finally I finish my quiz and hand it in. My classmates do the same, one by one, until Mr. Karas says the magic words: "It's lunchtime!"

If it isn't obvious, I like food. I *really* like it. Just thinking about it makes me happy.

When I eat too much food, my mom usually tells me to slow down. But slowing down is **SO** hard. It must be because I'm hitting a growth spurt every day.

Today's lunch is a ham and cheese sandwich with spinach and mayonnaise on whole wheat bread.

That's right. You heard me. **SPINACH.**

My dad says if I eat spinach, I'll get big, strong muscles like that cartoon character, Popeye. I don't really believe him, but if spinach will help me pick up a school bus with my bare hands, I'm willing to try it!

And speaking of cartoons, lunchtime is when Teddy and I sit with our friends Michael and Jason and talk about our favorite TV show: *Super Samurai from Outer Space!*

The show is about four Samurai brothers from ancient Japan who come across a meteorite that crash-landed in their village. When they touch the meteorite, they are transformed into super warrior astronauts.

Then they have the power to travel through the galaxy at the speed of light. Now their new mission is to fight mutants and monsters that want to destroy the universe.

"Hey, guys," Michael says. "How about we play an **EPICALLY AWESOME** game of Super Samurai during recess?"

Sometimes we like to pretend that we are each a Super Samurai. Some kids might think that is a little babyish. But those kids don't know what they are talking about. It's awesome.